Hidden Headlines:
A Seymour Clues Mystery

BRAVE
B O O K S

DOM-A-TRON

THE OLD ISLANDS

Burrycanter

Doomsdome

UTOPIA

Freedom Island

WIGGAMORE WOO

Rushington

SUMA SAVANNA

Hive H

Furenzy Park

Toke-A-Toke

Wonder Well

Capitol

Deserted Desert

Mushroom Village

Mt. Avalerif

RAKA RAIN FOREST

Sky Tree

Snapfast Meadow

CAR-A-LAGO COAST

Starlotte City

Gray Landing

Home of the Brave

Welcome to Freedom Island, Home of the Brave, where good battles evil and truth prevails. Join Seymour Clues and Mr. Mouse as they save Starlotte City and learn about the importance of free press. Complete the BRAVE Challenge at the end of the book to learn more!

Watch this video for an introduction to the story and BRAVE Universe!

Saga Three: Tubular
Book 3

**Hidden Headlines:
A Seymour Clues Mystery**

Saga Three: Tubular—Book 3

Hidden Headlines: A Seymour Clues Mystery
Copyright © 2023 by BRAVE BOOKS
All Rights Reserved

Book Illustrations © 2023 by Ali Elzeiny
Map Illustration © 2021 by Ali Elzeiny

Published by BRAVE BOOKS
www.BRAVEbooks.com

ISBN: 978-1-955550-38-3 (paperback)

First edition published in the USA in 2023 by BRAVE BOOKS

Printed in Canada

HIDDEN
HEADLINES:
A Seymour Clues Mystery

John Solomon and BRAVE BOOKS

Art by Ali Elzeiny

BRAVE
BOOKS

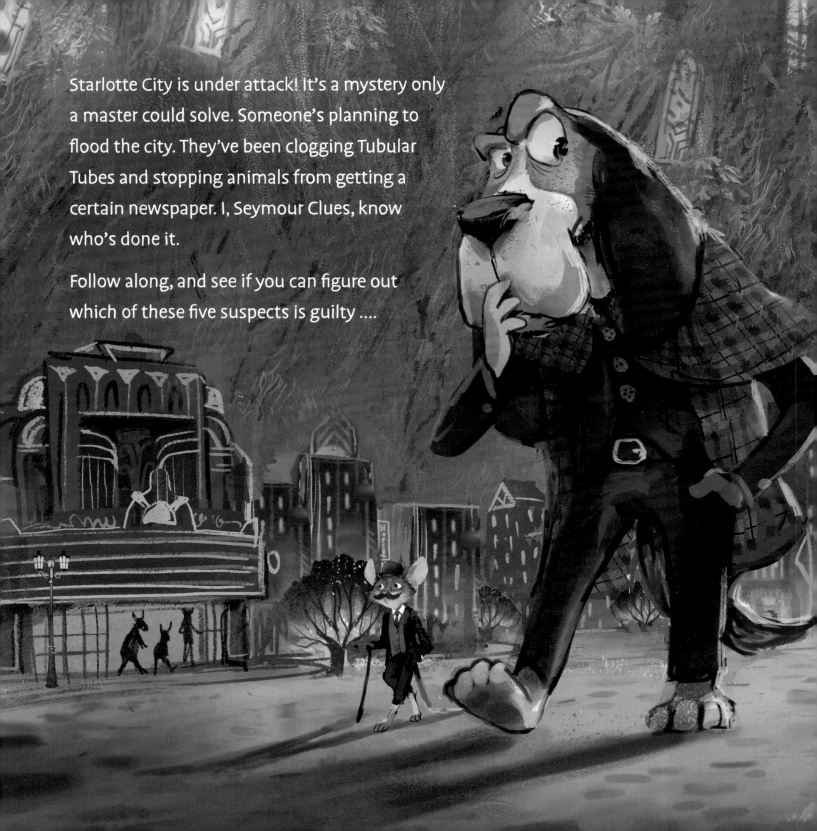

Starlotte City is under attack! It's a mystery only a master could solve. Someone's planning to flood the city. They've been clogging Tubular Tubes and stopping animals from getting a certain newspaper. I, Seymour Clues, know who's done it.

Follow along, and see if you can figure out which of these five suspects is guilty ....

Parrots

Mr. S

Penelope P

Karl

Chunk

It all started this morning when ...

A parrot stopped me and my detective partner, Mr. Mouse, on the street. "Have you heard? The Tubular Tubes are all clogged around the Hamster Headlines office! Why would the hamsters clog the tubes? What a mystery!" And then he flapped away.

The parrot asked a good question. Why **would** the hamsters clog the tubes? Could this be why I haven't seen the Hamster Headlines newspaper in a few weeks?

My thoughts were interrupted as a peacock breezed through my door.

Penelope P had become popular through Tubular, the system that animals use to share news and pictures across Freedom Island.

"Oh, Seymour Clues," she sighed. "I need your help! I heard the hamsters are clogging the Tubular Tubes. You have to stop them!"

I scratched my chin. "Hmm."

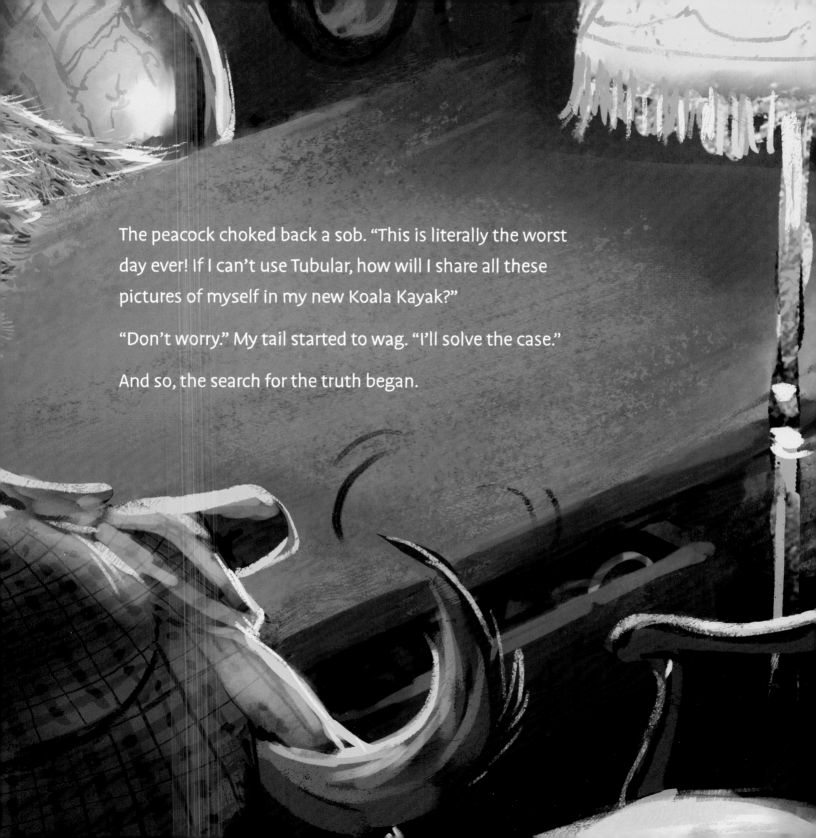

The peacock choked back a sob. "This is literally the worst day ever! If I can't use Tubular, how will I share all these pictures of myself in my new Koala Kayak?"

"Don't worry." My tail started to wag. "I'll solve the case."

And so, the search for the truth began.

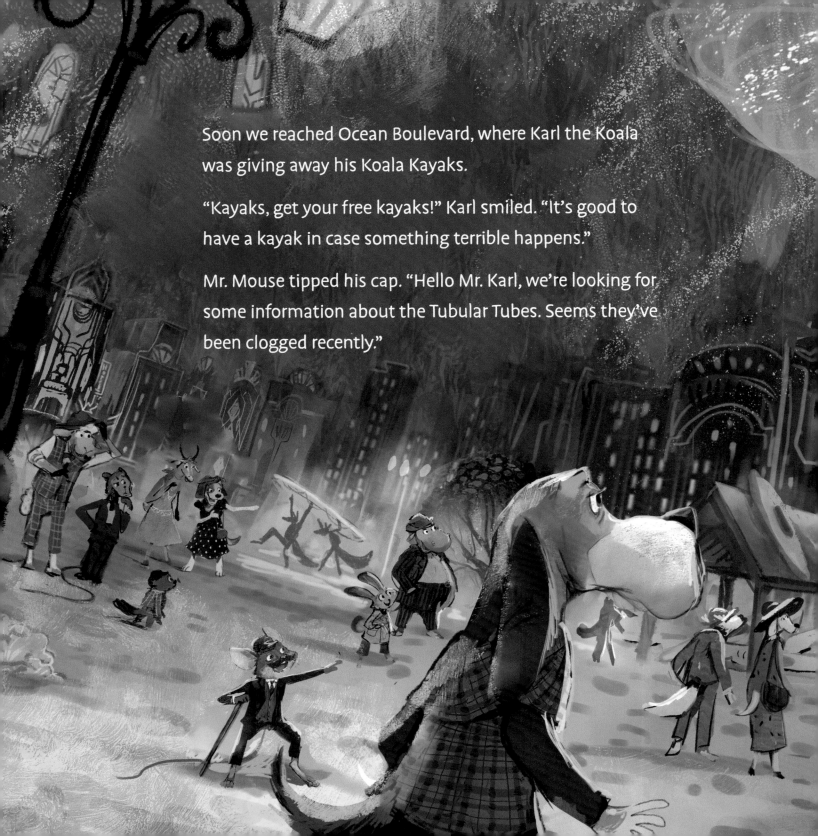

Soon we reached Ocean Boulevard, where Karl the Koala was giving away his Koala Kayaks.

"Kayaks, get your free kayaks!" Karl smiled. "It's good to have a kayak in case something terrible happens."

Mr. Mouse tipped his cap. "Hello Mr. Karl, we're looking for some information about the Tubular Tubes. Seems they've been clogged recently."

Karl replied, "I heard it was those hamsters clogging the tubes. Could be Chunk. He runs The Hamster Headlines, and has been upset ever since Mr. S told him to stop spreading his papers through Tubular. Anyway, do you want a kayak?"

"No, thank you." I waved goodbye, and we left to pay a visit to Mr. S. in the warehouse district of Starlotte City.

"Oh my!" The octopus jumped and started shifting the papers on his desk, "I wasn't expecting visitors ... How—how can I help you?"

"Why did you tell Chunk to stop spreading his news through the Tubular Tubes?" I asked.

"Well, I invented tubular, so of course I told him what I thought." Mr. S said. "It's no secret that Mr. Chunk and I have had our disagreements, but I would never stop him from sharing his newspapers."

"Can you tell us about the tubes getting clogged?" Mr. Mouse questioned.

"It's annoying." Mr. S frowned. "The hamsters continue to clog the tubes with long eucalyptus leaves, and I don't know why."

"Thank you, Mr. S," I said. "Sounds like I need to pay the hamsters a visit." So we headed to the small side of town.

When we reached the newsroom for The Hamster Headlines, Mr Mouse asked, "Where's Mr. Chunk?"

A hamster scurried up. "You're lookin' at him, chief. What can I do ya for?"

I glanced around his little office. "Why haven't I heard from The Hamster Headlines in a while?"

"Oh boy." The hamster sighed. "We can't get our news out because of all the tubes being stuffed with leaves near our newsroom. I've been tryin' to tell the animals that someone wants to flood the city, but—"

"Flood the city?" gasped Mr. Mouse. "Who would do such a terrible thing? And if you hamsters aren't clogging the tubes, then who is?"

I had heard enough. The case was closed.

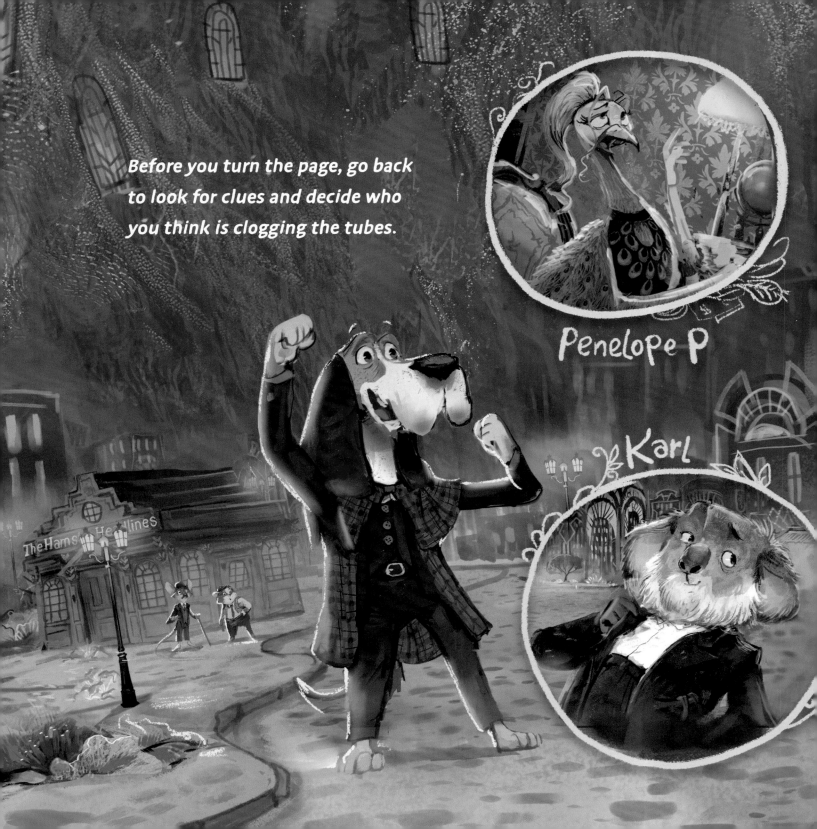

Before you turn the page, go back to look for clues and decide who you think is clogging the tubes.

Penelope P

Karl

Parrots

Chunk

Mr. S

"Karl!" I called across Ocean Boulevard.
"You're going to jail for a plot to flood
Starlotte City."

Karl's face hardened. "Flood the city?
What are you talking about?"

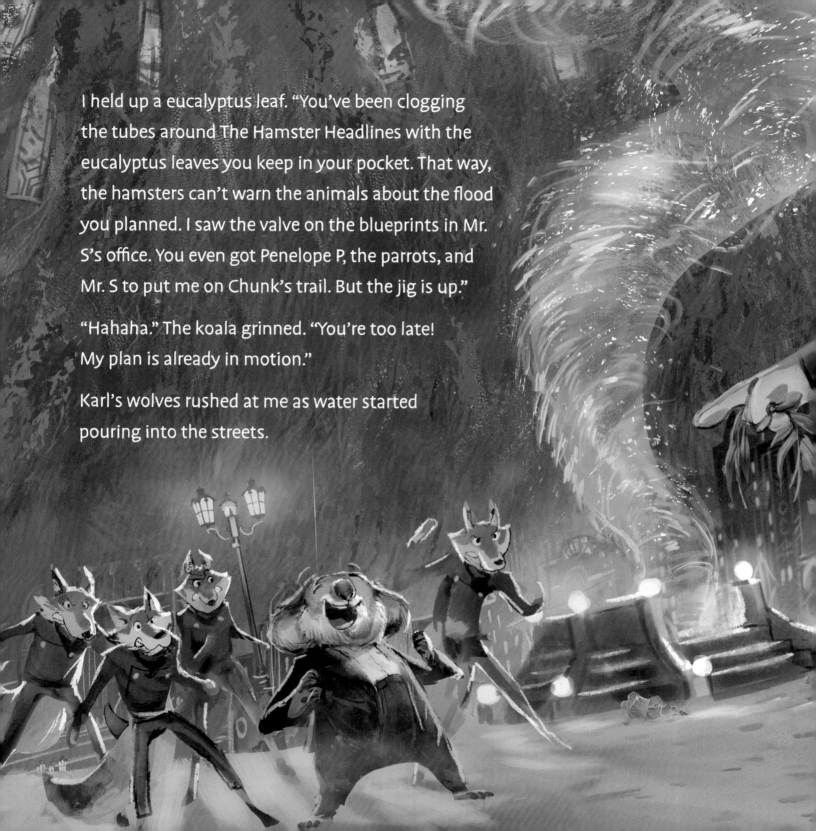

I held up a eucalyptus leaf. "You've been clogging the tubes around The Hamster Headlines with the eucalyptus leaves you keep in your pocket. That way, the hamsters can't warn the animals about the flood you planned. I saw the valve on the blueprints in Mr. S's office. You even got Penelope P, the parrots, and Mr. S to put me on Chunk's trail. But the jig is up."

"Hahaha." The koala grinned. "You're too late! My plan is already in motion."

Karl's wolves rushed at me as water started pouring into the streets.

With my black belt in karate, the wolves were no problem.

Karl the Koala climbed the nearest light pole. "Animals of Starlotte City, come and rely on me, and I can help you with my Koala Kayaks. Trust me, I am all you need!"

The animals rushed to get their free kayaks from Karl, thanking him over and over again. Karl smiled a big, sneaky smile, but what he didn't realize was ...

High in the seaweed dome,
Mr. Mouse and Chunk darted
through the tubes.

Mr. Mouse yelled, "The water valve
has to be here somewhere!"

They raced around a corner as water filled the city below. Chunk and Mr. Mouse struggled against a wave, reaching and stretching toward the big red valve.

Suddenly, the water slowed to a trickle,
then a drip, then it dried up all together.

My two little partners scurried out of a nearby tube
soaked and out of breath. "Phew! That was a close one."

"No!" stomped Karl. "You were supposed to need me so
I could save you and become ruler of this city!"

I turned to speak to the animals of Starlotte City, "Listen everyone, Karl was stopping the Hamster Headlines. But it was because of the hamsters that we were able to stop the flood. We must let voices be heard. When we let a few animals decide what should or shouldn't be said, terrible things can happen."

Chunk returned to The Hamster Headlines newsroom. From that day forward, his newspaper was able to get to everyone, and all the animals knew what was really happening in their glittering city.

THE HAMSTER HEADLINES

Issue 3

The Big Scoop from a Little Starlotte City Office

TUBULAR TUBES CLEARED THANKS TO SEYMOUR, MR. MOUSE, AND CHUNK

Does Penelope P have a Sister?

One such Penelope P fan claims to be related to the popular Tubular user. "I really am her number 1 fan. I copy her looks, talk the same way, and even share similar photos through Tubular. I mean, we're like sisters!" We attempted to reach out to Penelope P regarding this possible family connection, but all we received in return was a signed selfie.

BRAVE CADETS,

In a follow-up interview, Seymour asked Mr. S, founder of Tubular, if he had any connections with Karl about the recent flooding in Starlotte City. Complete the three missions below to help prove Karl is guilty!

- Update your map with the Karl and flag stickers included.

- Help Seymour in the BRAVE Challenge, and celebrate your victory with an epic reward.

- Can you find a pair of scissors, a teapot, and a wrench in the story?

Seymour Clues is counting on you! Are you ready to be BRAVE?

The Great Raka Rapids Race Coming Up!

We all love the summer. It's the time for surfing some waves, playing with friends, and eating watermelon. However, nothing excites me more than the Raka Rapids Race, held in the Raka Rainforest. Along with a sturdy raft, racers will have to rely on their strength, their smarts, and their speed in this fun-filled water sport. I look forward to seeing this year's participants, especially with rumors about Team BRAVE potentially joining in.

THE BRAVE CHALLENGE

INTRODUCING...
JOHN SOLOMON

John Solomon is the founder of the news agency, *Just The News*, where he serves today as the Editor-in-Chief. Solomon believes that the news and other social networks should be truthful and he is constantly striving to provide trustworthy information to his readers, both through his news agency and his podcast, John Solomon Report. Solomon partnered with BRAVE Books to create, *Hidden Headlines*, a book on the First Amendment right of freedom of press.

JOHN SUGGESTS:

"Enjoy this BRAVE Challenge that we put together for the whole family. This is a great opportunity to teach your kids about free press."

Freedom of Press: a promise in the U.S. Constitution that the government will not stop journalists, reporters, or any other news agency from publishing the news or their thoughts about it.

INTRODUCTION

Starlotte City is in danger! If your team can put more points on the scoreboard than Karl, you have won the challenge and saved Starlotte City! To get started, grab a sheet of paper and a pencil, and draw a scoreboard like the one shown.

Before starting Game #1, choose a prize for winning. For example ...

BRAVE Cadets	Karl
ⅢⅢ I	Ⅲ

- Going to the pool
- Having your favorite tasty treat
- Playing a board game
- Whatever gets your kiddos excited!

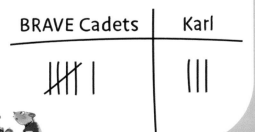

GAME #1 - PUZZLED & SPEECHLESS

LESSON

The Freedom of Press allows any amount of voices to share their viewpoints.

OBJECTIVE

The animals of Starlotte City are distracted by the opinions of others rather than coming up with their own! BRAVE Cadets, show them the importance of everyone sharing their opinions.

MATERIALS

Scissors, a piece of paper, colored markers, and a timer.

INSTRUCTIONS

Setup:

1. Send the cadets out of the room while parents prepare the game.

2. Choose one of the 2 puzzles from the illustrations depending on the cadets ages.

BRAVE TIP

If the cadets are under 5 years old, use puzzle #1.
Use puzzle #2 otherwise.

3. Recreate the image below on a sheet of paper. Color the pieces and then cut out the puzzle pieces.

4. Mix up the puzzle before calling the cadets back into the room.

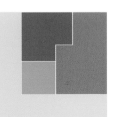

Puzzle #1
Answer Key

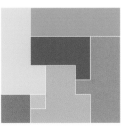

Puzzle #2
Answer Key

Game Play:

5. Set up a 3 minute timer.

6. The youngest cadet is the only cadet allowed to speak and look at the puzzle on page 44.

7. The youngest cadet cannot point or gesture and can only use words for giving direction.

8. That cadet will guide the other cadets to move the pieces to where they need to be. The other cadets cannot move the pieces unless told to do so by the youngest cadet.

9. If the other cadets talk during the game, they will lose points.

SCORING

Roll the die for Karl's score. The cadets receive 6 points if they complete the puzzle in under 1 minute, 4 points in under 2 minutes, and 2 points in under 3 minutes. If any of the cadets, not including the youngest cadets, talk during the game, they lose a point.

TIME

Set a 3 minute timer before starting the puzzle.

ONE CHILD MODIFICATION

Have the parents play with the cadet. The cadet will be the one to lead the parents to complete the puzzle.

TALK ABOUT IT

1. Who is the press in Starlotte City? Who is the press in real life?

2. What does freedom of press mean? (See definition on page 43.)

JOHN SUGGESTS:

"The press reports the news. When you hear the words 'free press,' it means that we have the freedom to write or share what we want without government involvement. Free press is important because without it, the truth might become suppressed."

3. In the game, one of the cadets had to lead the others to complete a puzzle. Was it hard when only one person could speak? Why is it important that we hear others' opinions?

4. In the story, the citizens of Starlotte City weren't sharing their opinions but were distracted by the opinions of the parrots and Penelope P. Why is it good to hear the opinions of others around us? When do you think it becomes dangerous?

    "Know this, my beloved brothers: let every person be
    quick to hear, slow to speak, slow to anger."
    James 1:19 (ESV)

5. In the story, the parrots wrote news articles that were lies. Is it a good thing to have freedom in what we can write? Why can't we have complete freedom?

GAME #2 - PRESSED FOR TIME

LESSON

When free press is suppressed, people will be blind to the whole truth.

OBJECTIVE

Karl is planning to stop the animals from knowing the truth about his plot by clogging up the tubes around the Hamster Headlines! BRAVE Cadets, help the hamsters send more of their newspapers out to the animals before Karl can clog the tubes.

MATERIALS

1 empty basket,
1 white sock ball,
1 black sock ball,
and a timer.

INSTRUCTIONS

1. Place the basket across the room and have the cadets stand in a single file line starting around 5 feet away from the basket. Have the parent stand around 8 feet away from the basket. Make sure to mark the place where both teams are standing.

2. Give the white sock ball to the first cadet in line and the black sock ball to the parent. (The white sock ball represents the hamsters' newspapers and the black sock ball represents Karl's eucalyptus leaves.)

3. Start a 3 minute timer. The first cadet and parent will try to throw their sock ball into the basket.

4. Once they throw their sock ball, they must run to grab it and race back to their marked spot. The cadet will pass the sock ball to the next cadet while the parent continues to throw from their marked spot.

BRAVE TIP

Make sure to keep count of how many sock balls both teams make during the game!

SCORING

Both teams earn a point for every basket made.

TIME

Set a 3 minute timer before beginning the game.

TALK ABOUT IT

1. In the game you had to help the hamsters send out as many newspapers as you could before Karl could clog up the tubes. What did the different colored socks represent in the game?

2. Who hid the truth about the flood in the story? Why were Chunk's newspaper articles about the flood suppressed?

3. Parents, give an example of distracting or lying stories in the news and other media platforms. Why do people want to hide the truth?

"For nothing is hidden that will not be made manifest, nor is anything secret that will not be known and come to light."

Luke 8:17 (ESV)

4. Why is it dangerous if we can't hear the truth of what's happening around us?

5. How can we search for the truth daily?

TALLY UP THE POINTS TO SEE IF YOU WON!

FINAL THOUGHTS FROM JOHN

The First Amendment in the US Constitution states that the government can not make any laws that stops the freedom of speech. This law is extremely important for our country because without the freedom to share thoughts, ideas, and true events, we would be blind to some important truths. Sadly in today's world, some of the information that we see is twisted and is meant to trick the public. Because of this, we must be careful when we receive information and avoid immediately believing what we see or hear.